THE GRIM REAPER

LOOKBOOK

RIYA AARINI

The Grim Reaper Lookbook

Select images licensed from Shutterstock

Select images created with the assistance of AI under the creative direction of the author

ISBN: 978-1-956496-80-2 (paperback)

ISBN: 978-1-956496-81-9 (hardcover)

ISBN: 978-1-956496-82-6 (eBook)

CONTENTS

Welcome

This is the grim reaper. I'm here to discuss what no one ever talks about: my style. It's often overlooked, as people generally scramble away from me at first sight. *Humph*. I think it has to do with my fashion choices, which are not entirely *my* decisions alone.

If I weren't so frumpy, maybe folks wouldn't scream for their lives—or about the end of their lives—every time I made an entrance. I basically appear out of nowhere, like a menacing shadow out to grab your soul, which is technically what I do. Well, that's the way things are for now.

I do have an appointment with my stylist, who's responsible for my look, and will be insisting we make some changes to my guise. (You don't know how awfully long it takes to get on her calendar. She's booked hundreds of years out, serving the middle-realm as an independent consultant.)

In the meantime, we'll be visiting some looks I'd like to see added to my wardrobe in the near future as well as a few tech-driven conveniences to make the job of today's grim reaper easier.

Until we officially meet, *memento mori.*

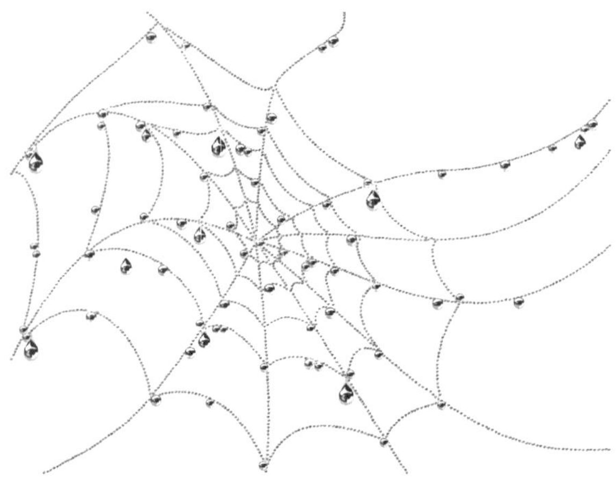

1. Haute Couture

My clients are discerning. Most souls don't want to be greeted by a mysterious phantom dressed in black tatters. *Ugh.* I'll admit, I don't like doing my job in this shabby getup either. It feels as if I'm lower than the lowest, the ugly, brown coffee ring under the mug, the slimy rinds at the bottom of the garbage disposal, the damaging fatbergs in the drain pipe. What I need is an outfit made with the finest craftsmanship, luxury materials that push the boundaries of fashion—haute couture, my friends.

Imagine your soul being harvested by a phantom of exquisite taste, wearing an outfit meticulously sewn that lifts me out from the crowd. You'd never forget a reaper dressed in high fashion.

As a spirit with the most peculiar task in the universe, I entertain unique tastes in clothing. As such, it's fitting that I dress in a style that reflects my individual preferences. The exceptional garment I wear must be handmade by skilled artisans, dedicated to making the reaper shine with hundreds of hours of untiring work. What results is an outfit of unparalleled quality, exclusive to the reaper alone.

The arrival of a reaper dressed in haute couture would generate buzz around death. Maybe I'd inspire trends, motivate designers to experiment with fabrics, patterns, colors, ideas. I'd turn the fashion industry upside down. Who wouldn't want to dress like a reaper who's precociously elevated his style?

Reaper is my name, and innovation is my game. After I consult my stylist about potential new looks, I'm sure to descend, robed in unmatched glamour. You just might be impressed to see me.

Today's grim reaper struts in style.

An exotic alternative to showcase my worldliness—and otherworldliness.

Lending swankiness to the business of death.

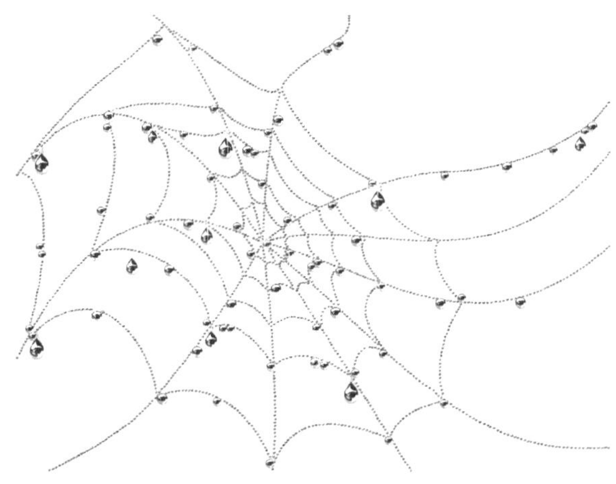

2. Fuzzy Slippers

I'm perpetually barefoot. It's agonizing. Despite being entirely made of bone, my feet have needs, too, and appreciate soft, cushiony feels every now and then. I've been on my feet for centuries, rowing souls to the next world, without even a pair of boots to cushion my steps. It's time things change.

All I ask for is a nice pair of fuzzy slippers. In pastel blue or mint green. Maybe cute bunny slippers or bear claws or cuddly cat slippers. Not much to ask, is it? My feet would be snug, surrounded by faux fur or the finest plush on Earth. I'd lean back in my recliner, placing my feet on the footrest, and enjoy the sense of utter relaxation. When it's cold out—and it gets frigid in the middle realm—the fuzzy slippers would keep my feet toasty. Even when walking into the restroom, my house slippers would protect my feet from bacteria, fungi, and, in short, infections. No one needs a grim reaper to take sick leave because he caught a bug. Letting souls hang in limbo until I felt better would be ridiculous.

I'm on my feet a lot, and a little softness underfoot would reduce the stress on my joints and the inevitable foot pain I experience—which I grudgingly push through every nanosecond. Why else do you think I wear a persistent scowl? It's the fuzzy slippers that'll wipe that frown off my face. So how 'bout a pair?

Just chillin' in front of the tube.

Nothin's cozier than fuzzy slippers on a Saturday morning.

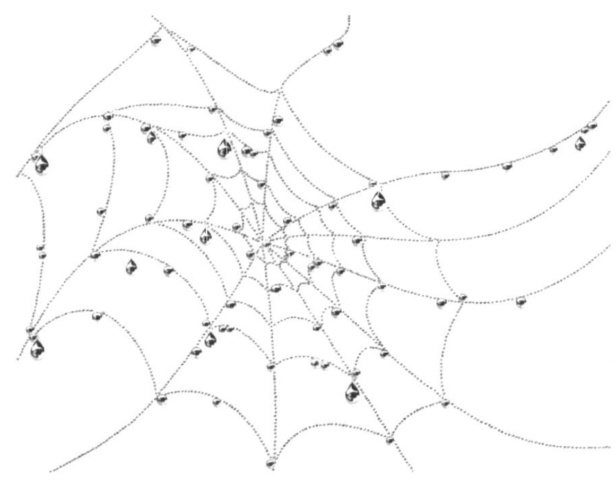

3. Blinged-Out Scythe

My scythe is a seven-hundred-year-old chunk of dull metal. Do you know how many souls I've harvested with this thing? It's getting old, literally and figuratively. This worn blade needs an upgrade, something sharper, eye-catching, even dazzling. Who'd want their soul harvested with a blunt blade? *Ouch*. No, I aim to please and promote comfort—in impeccable style. The solution? A blinged-out scythe—a diamond-studded blade, glimmering brighter than the golden sun at midday. Awestruck is the name of this game. My clients would drop their mouths open, utterly dazed by the bling. A swanky reaper decked out in bling is a showstopper. The lives of my clients may have stopped—but the show goes on in the next world, courtesy of a blinged-out scythe that does the reaping with one clean, iced-out slice.

A bit of bling on the accoutrements.

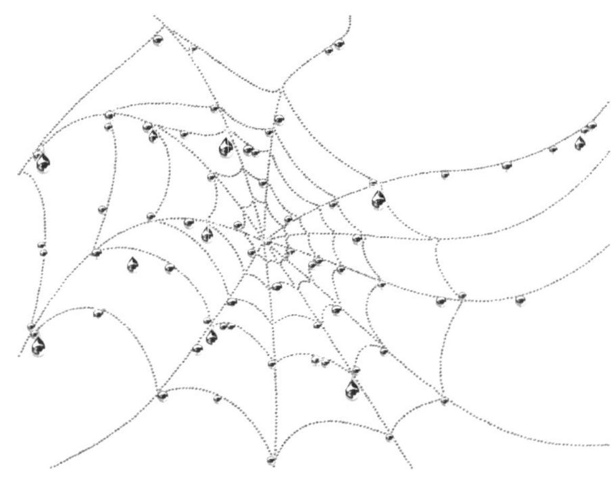

4. Designer Suit

I may not be haute couture based on my current look, but I do love upscale fashion. Honestly, I abhor dragging souls around to the esteemed next realm in this drab, barely-there outfit, handed down to me in the fourteenth century. The Black Plague killed a lot, including my elevated sense of style. But I aim to get it back. Death may never change, but as the grim reaper in Death's service, I have the strong urge to rotate my outfits. You do, so why can't I? I almost never pick up two souls wearing the same outfit. Every soul is unique, and so are their garments. I deserve fashion freedom just the same. I am the deliverer of souls, after all, and should dress for this worthy part.

This means, for me, and you may be a little surprised, a red designer suit, sewn with fine fabric, complete with a black tuxedo shirt underneath. Add an embroidered black pocket square jutting out of my front *barchetta* pocket for a touch of elegance. A shawl lapel, soft as satin, would be nice. A single button is all I need for closure; and, if the button is covered in satin, all the better. That's sophistication, grim reaper style. Extra points if the suit is luxury and handmade. I might fudge a few numbers and up the years of the brave soul who's willing to customize a fiery red designer suit for yours truly.

Death is inevitable. Can't we dress it up a little?

Definitely an upgrade from the status quo.

A little dinner, dancing, and death.

Making an unforgettable first impression.

Me and my swagger.

This outfit shows respect for the whole death thing, right?

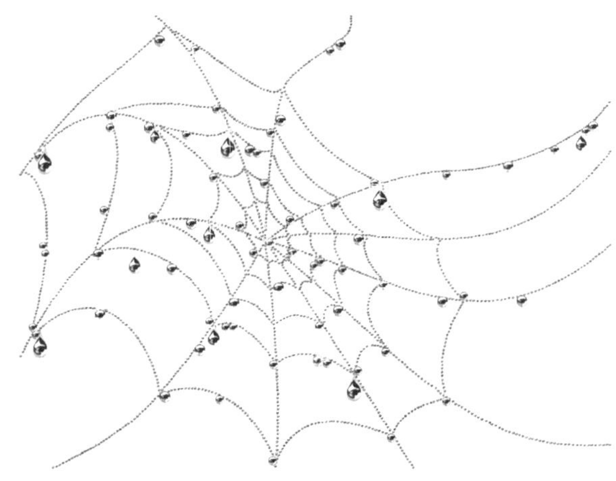

5. Scented Candles

Lighting candles at funerals is a popular practice—but one I'm not particularly fond of. The flame is supposed to guide the departed to the afterlife. Hey, that's my job! I don't like the idea of competing with a teensy-weensy candle, but I do see its value in enhancing my existence.

I'm referring to scented candles. I'm considering ordering a dozen of these to place around my bathtub as I soak after a busy month, like December or January, when the peak number of souls decide to take the leap and sojourn to the other side. Great minds think alike, which explains why these folks choose to depart around the same time, like lemmings jumping off a cliff en masse.

Bubble baths are incredibly relaxing during these preposterously hectic times. Candles make bathtimes all the more soothing. Scented ones, like peppermint, create a relaxing night of aromatherapy. After pondering the profound quote scribbled on the candle label, I'd stare into the flickering flame and engage in a bit of mindfulness. There's no better way for a reaper to unwind.

A candle doubly serves as a versatile gift for deserving souls. Death is the ideal occasion for gift-giving, and with so many sizes, scents, and colors, finding the perfect candle for a soul is a cinch. I'd go so far as to say giving a candle to harried souls is a thoughtful gesture. I'd personalize the candles with the words "You're dead to me," and give them out like candy on Halloween. It'd create a cozy ambiance on my boat, comforting souls and elevating their mood, as they travel to the other side wrapped in warmth.

I think it's a nice touch.

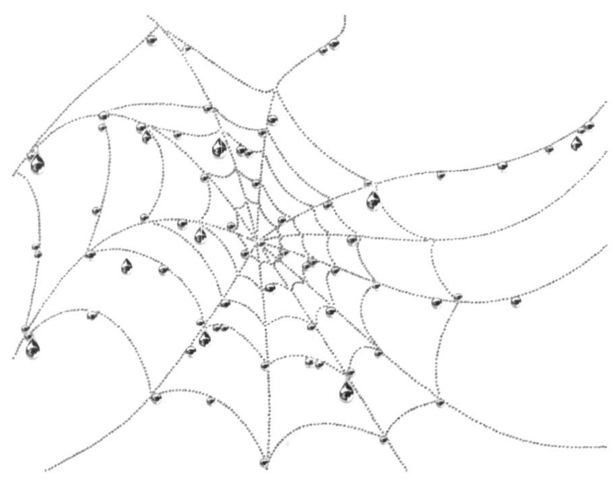

6. New Robe

This hooded, black robe is my downfall. It's the first thing people see other than my bony grin. It's been my go-to outerwear for centuries. Unlike regular folks, I can't just sell it off at a garage sale to be repurposed. Why? Would you buy a torn-up robe that's been around the world a gazillion times, never been properly laundered (who in the next realm even owns a washer-dryer combo?), and that could fall to pieces the second you laid your hands on it? *Humph*. This robe needs an upgrade. If my stylist disagrees, she best curate looks for a new phantasm. I'm not having one more unearthly second of this frayed disaster. Along with my other archaic elements of style, the ragged robe might be among the reasons people flee from me.

It's time for new garb.

There's so much to choose from: a delicate silk kimono, a shawl collar robe, or a short robe. *Ugh*, a short robe would reveal my knobby knee bones, so I'll pass on that. People are afraid of me already; I don't need my bony knees to scare them off before I get ahold of them. There's a reason the grim reaper is fully covered from skull to toe bones.

But silk? Ah, the fineness of silk against my cold, ashen bones would feel like a luxury. What about a cashmere robe? Exquisite! Maybe handmade and red, with a floral pattern? A bit of fringe along the bottom edge would give my look a bohemian aesthetic.

I'd definitely go for a color different than my signature one. Black represents ominous darkness, but I transport souls to the light! So black isn't a fair color. A cool, sapphire blue? The options are endless!

Do you dig the fringe?

Timeless, right? I insisted on the hood for that recognizable grim reaper flair.

It's symbolic of the good fortune of being delivered to the idyllic afterlife.

Oh, this wasn't supposed to be in my lookbook! I rolled out of bed and threw this thing on, just before making myself a cup of coffee. Hmm?

See what I mean about the knobby knees?

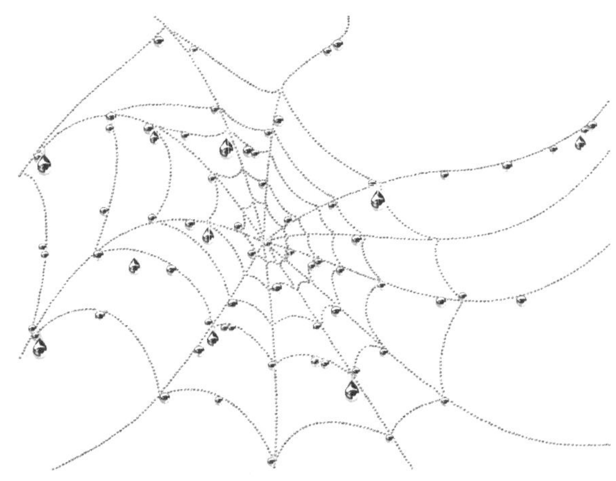

7. Wig Collection

It's time to reinvent myself. I've thought up a few new looks that express my individuality and have the potential to sway others' perceptions of me in the right direction. Come on, I'm bald, with nothing atop my skull to gloat about. I don't deal with pomade or pricey sprays to set a glamorous look. In a way, it's convenient and a major time saver. But I'm in a new phase and want to express this dramatic change.

Enter wigs—wigs I can switch out as I please. You never know if the reaper will show up as a vibrant redhead, a mysterious dark-haired phantom, a graying gent, or a bubbly blonde.

A fine wig that rests over my bare skull would serve me well, boosting my self-esteem and confidence. I dare say the right wig has the potential to influence how others perceive my reliability. In the game of soul harvesting, dependability is a critical factor. Hair so deftly fulfills that need.

What type of wig would add sizzle to my style? The endless variations give my butterflies!

Let's start with the obvious: powder wigs from the seventeenth century. European aristocrats paraded around in these elaborate hairdos, garnering attention and admiration from their peers. I might take a cue and sport one myself. Here I am trying one on.

How's it look? It's wondrous how a few strategically placed goat hairs elevate my status instantly. Gives death a sort of dignity, doesn't it?

Trading the customary baldness for a lush, black wig evoking King Charles II vibes. Adds an air of aristocracy to my guise, eh?

A bleached blond mullet wig from the eighties.

I'm more approachable, right?

Cowabunga! How'd you like your soul to be picked up by a reaper wearing one of these? Changes the whole soul harvesting experience, doesn't it?

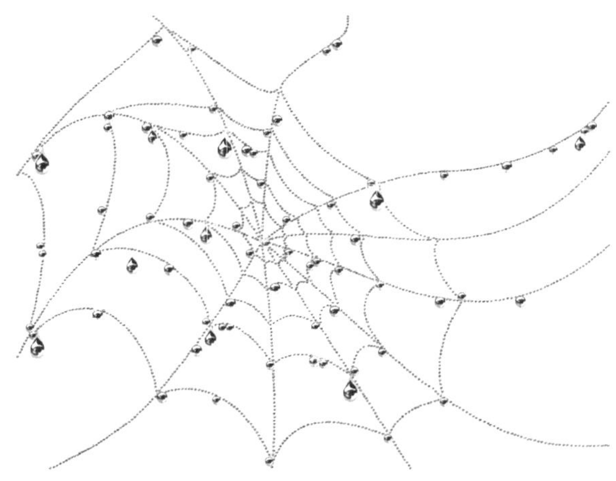

8. Crown

I hold the unpleasant status as a lowly reaper, a phantasmagoric being whom no one thinks much of, just a worthless shadow, here and gone in a fleeting second. Honestly, being thought of so poorly is heartbreaking. It must be the hood. It serves no purpose other than to conceal my luminous skull—a flawless skull that deserves to be shown off, even admired.

One minor accessory can achieve such a worthy goal: a crown! A golden, gleaming crown, encrusted with brilliant jewels and oh so delightfully heavy to wear—the mark of true royalty. I'd be regaled as the king of death, rather than a curmudgeonly, impoverished, thin-as-bones reaper. I don't know why my stylist gave me a hood in the first place. It's not like I get the shivers. My bones are perpetually cold, and no headwear can fix that. But a crown? A crown delivers the impression I hope for: a magnificent aristocrat who swoops down to steal folks away from the worries of life and transport them to a new realm flooded with peace and overwhelming joy. Yep, a nice crown will do just that.

Forget the scythe. The crown gives me legitimacy.

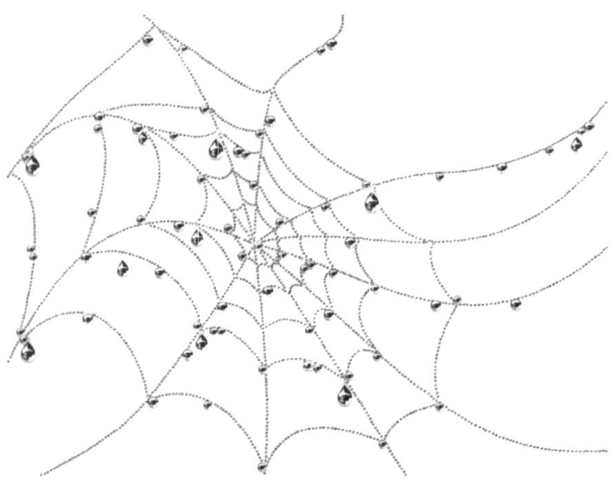

9. Bluebirds

Red-faced, I admit to feeling a little competitive with crows. These highly intelligent birds are seen in various cultures as guides to the afterlife. Ahem, that's *my* role. Crows, man, they got to go. Sure, they're viewed as harbingers of death—but so am I! No crow precariously navigates a fragile rowboat to the next world and gives souls a friendly toodle-oo as they step off to the land of eternal light. Crows might be messengers of death, but that's because they have wings! I'm just not that fortunate to be fitted with aerial capabilities. It's time for change.

I'm thinking something more cheerful than, blah, crows—a replacement that sings rather than caws, a light instead of a dark, a flit of wings instead of a thunderous flap. What omen is this, you ask? What could possibly replace crows, when they've symbolized death since the dinosaurs, from whom they directly descend?

Why, bluebirds, of course! The birds' melodic song would give death a more welcome reception. They'd symbolize the new beginnings souls experience in the next world. All souls get a fresh start once they set foot in the eternal realm; so, why not bring to the scene the hope these charming warblers deliver? Bluebirds would definitely boost my reputation, even infusing the death process with ideas of renewal, good luck, and harmony. Who isn't outright lucky when they get to meet me? I'm quite the guy. And with little bluebirds flitting around me, it's proof.

Fluttering around death are hope and renewal, attributes of the glorious afterlife.

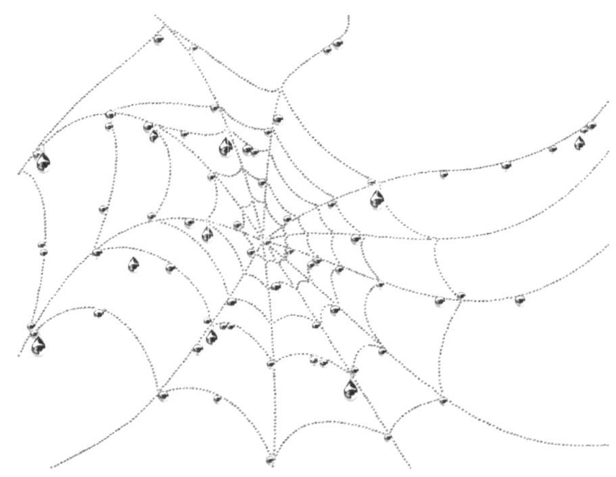

10. GPS

Granted, not all souls are picked up in easy-to-spot locations. Some areas are remote, out of the way, and require enormous fortitude to reach. Whether a soul is harvested from the topmost branches of a Brazil nut tree in the thick Amazon jungle (don't ask; it's happened) or deep inside the belly of a lion in a parched savannah, they're not always quick to find. I've had to don scuba gear on some occasions to reach the mouths of caves in uninhabited islands and learn to scale cliffs. Anyway, it's not unheard of for souls to linger uncomfortably in limbo for longer than expected when I have to make enormous effort to navigate to their impossible-to-discover final resting spot.

I've relied on paper maps through the ages for this very purpose. But largescale maps have been a hassle to manage, especially on gusty days and dark nights. It should be a no-brainer that today's reaper needs a satellite GPS tracking system. If folks use it to find their parked cars, by golly, a reaper should have access to one to find lost souls.

I'd call it a GPS soul tracker. The tracker would give me real-time data as to the whereabouts of a soul in their precise final moment. It would even provide the distance traveled, making it extra convenient for me to determine how long it'd take to be at point A to collect a soul and then at point B in the nick of time to serve another. For the sake of convenience, I prefer a portable soul tracker that's small enough to fit in my pocket. Is that too much to ask?

Now, how do I work this thing?

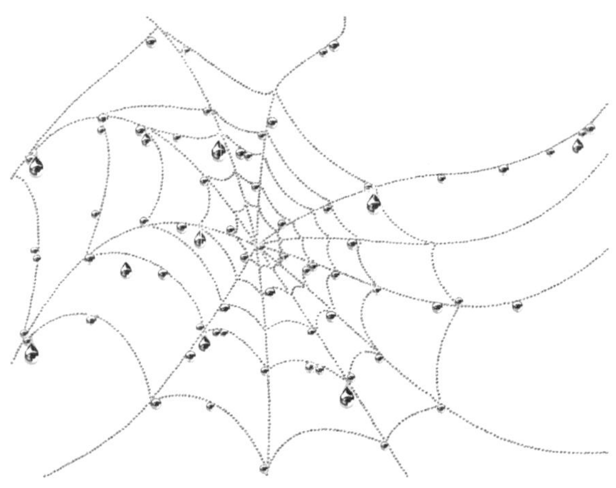

11. Speedboat

I've been rowing a rickety, old wooden boat for centuries. It comes with a chipped oar and an age-old lantern with a wick that I'm sure will shrivel up when I need it most. The river is dark, and even I can get lost in the gloomy fog that descends as I row my clients to the other side. I wouldn't want to lose my way and mistakenly row a client back to earthly existence. That would be an utter fiasco. What would people think?

Then there's the holes I've patched up in the boat, the warped wood, and...

Enough! I can't go on rowing this floating hazard. What I need is an upgrade: a speedboat, sleek and gleaming white, featuring a premium sound system, a sun deck, and an engine so powerful it'd transport my clients to the to the next realm in the blink of an eye. A fast boat is a reaper's dream machine. It's calling my name!

With plenty up for sale, it shouldn't be too troublesome to find the perfect one. I could take time out of my busy schedule to go boat hunting. It's not impossible to make a reaper's onerous existence a little easier. Now is it?

In my Zen zone.

I'm in complete control. It's fabulous!

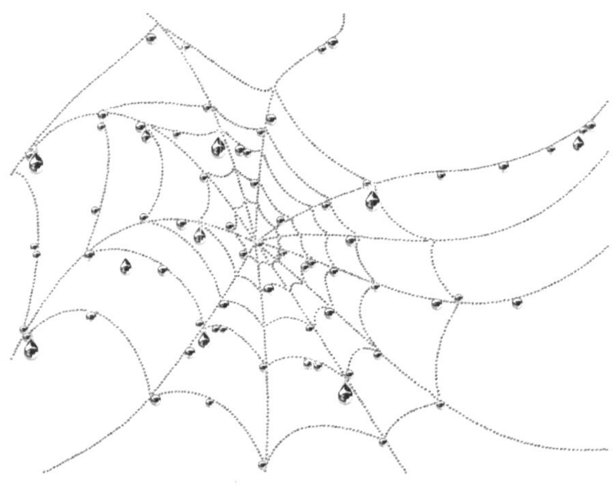

12. Pet Gerbil

Being a little rough around the edges, I think a pet to offset my starkness might cheer up the despairing souls I collect and add a little amusement to my grisly task. Something small, not too high maintenance, and that's active night or day—considering my wild job takes me around the globe at all hours. I've contemplated a puppy or even a lizard, but both require a major time investment. I'm already committed to picking up souls 24/7, so anything high-maintenance is a deal breaker.

It dawned on me after roaming and observing the earthly sphere that a teensy furball might just do it for me. A gerbil. Yes, a tiny golden-furred gerbil to sit on my shoulder. He'd brim with personality, as I made my rounds. I'd name him Elvis or, if she's a gal, Priscilla. Maybe give him a tummy rub every now and then as he supervises the harvesting of souls. I see the joyful look on the souls' faces when they see my pet gerbil munching carrots on my shoulder.

Elvis would be a constant companion, being the adorable social animal he is. I wouldn't mind his show of affection, burrowing into my hood when I stumble upon gruesome scenes requiring my immediate presence. A playful critter, Elvis would entertain me on slow days; I'd watch him making wacky decisions, playing with his toys, or running mindlessly in his wheel. After a few rides to the other side with me, we'd form a tight bond, relieving my lonesome days and dreary nights. I'd return the favor by cuddling with my curious best bud, maybe let souls snuggle up to him too. Eh, who ever thought owning a gerbil could be so rewarding?

You might meet Elvis when I appear. Bring carrots.

Who couldn't love a face like this?

Elvis. He's part of the family.

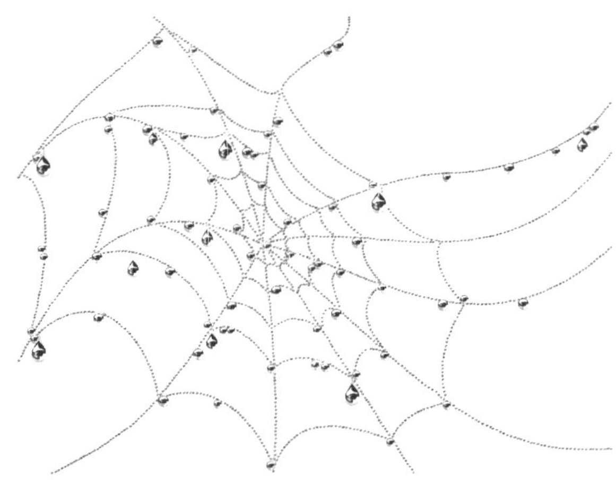

13. Hat Collection

I get the practicality of a hood. It protects the back of my neck bones from wind, cold, and harmful UV rays. I can safely say I've never been sunburned or frostbitten in that neck of the woods. The hood serves as protection, an important garment to keep me comfortable as I weather extreme heat, subfreezing temperatures, and fiercely windy destinations. But my hood is so...blah. Drab, boring. I'm kicking my headwear up a notch. Maybe try a new style, a new color, or ditch the hood altogether.

I take my cue from the Kentucky Derby—where hats are the ultimate showstoppers. I'd like a piece of that outlandish glamour and become the main attraction myself. Show off a little luxury, my impeccable taste, and a whole lot of flair. Grim reaper plus flair? Those two words haven't gone together for the last seven centuries. But times are changing. Ditching my hood is the way to play the game today.

Now I'm no crazy hat reaper, but I do intend on building my collection.

A taco hat, reminiscent of Napoleon's bicorne hat with two corners, would brighten the day of any soul I harvested. Kudos to the first soul who sees me in one. As I sport the playful headwear, maybe death wouldn't seem so gruesome.

I might strut around the middle realm wearing a cityscape atop my skull, or go all out with spirals of pink foam. I wouldn't mind a pair of flamingos sitting on my skull, decked in miniature hats themselves. I do like my tea, and a picture-perfect hat is a tea kettle pouring delicate florals into a stack of teacups.

The creative possibilities are boundless. Have a look for yourself.

Just showcasing my personality.

No, I'm not the donut vendor.

Fit right in, don't I?

There's no conversation starter like this one.

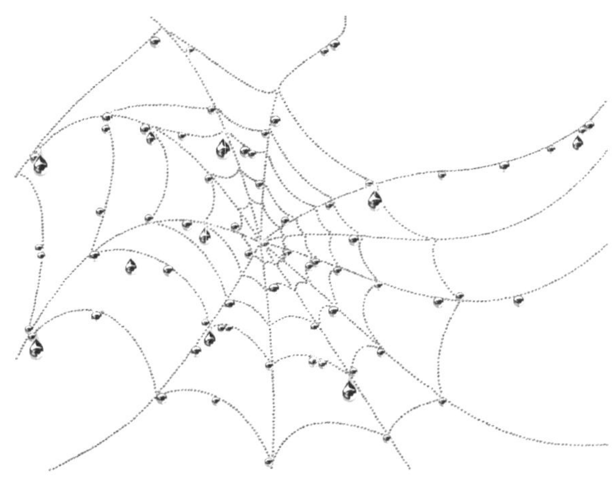

14. Motorcycle

Instead of the shabby boat folks are accustomed to seeing me in, a motorcycle is far more in keeping with the times. Not any motorcycle—but one that offers performance and a comfy sidecar for souls. They're already filled with angst, not knowing what to expect on the other side. But a nice little sidecar might ease their fright. They'd hop in, buckle up, and be ready for the trip to the next world. Of course, I'd hand the souls a helmet to protect them from—well, they're already dead. But it'd still be a nice gesture.

Off I'd go, transporting clients to the other side via a wild motorcycle ride, down the dusty, deserted highway of life, clocking over 150 miles per hour. The speed of a motorcycle is superior to that of a boat, even an upgraded one that sails a mere sixty miles per hour. The swiftness to the eternal realm is to my advantage.

People would point and say, "There's the reaper with his thrilling ride!"

I'd be a daring caper on two wheels, *ahem*, four, if you count the sidecar. The fast ride would give souls an adrenaline-pumping experience they'd never forget. A sleek motorcycle gives me the reputation I should be known for: fast and furious!

Buckle up. You'll thank me later.

I could own an entire fleet of motorcycles, dubbed the "Wheels to Eternity"!

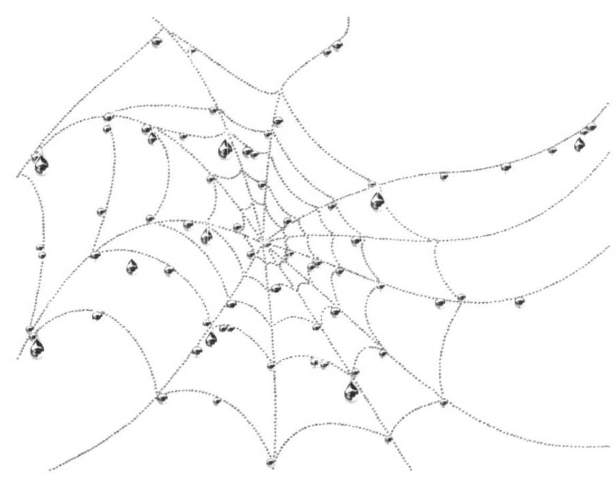

15. Headlamp

Lanterns have been my source of light for hundreds of years. They've illuminated my paths as I crossed the River Styx and climbed mountainous terrain to reach the peaks where hikers took their last breaths. But please, a lantern? You can't imagine how difficult it is to hold a lantern with one hand and try to climb Mount Everest with the other. The flame blows out on windy days, adding to my frustration. Not to mention, a lantern is a major fire hazard, especially when I accidentally leave it near flammable materials, like decaying trees. Plus, cleaning the wick is a pain. Given all the technology available, it's obvious I need something that makes my task less perilous and more expedient.

Something like a headlamp. Wearing the headlamp, I'd have both hands free. The light allows me to peruse intricate maps when souls are hovering in complex geographic areas in the stark dead of night. I can even set up camp without needing to hold a light source. Ever try to open a can of baked beans with one hand without spilling the contents? While navigating trails, the wide beam lights up my path, helping me see my surroundings far more clearly than with a meager lantern. You don't know how many times I've nearly fallen to my second death while traversing hazardous cliffs at midnight. I say, out with the old, and in with the new. Now that's a bright idea!

Two thumbs up to technology!

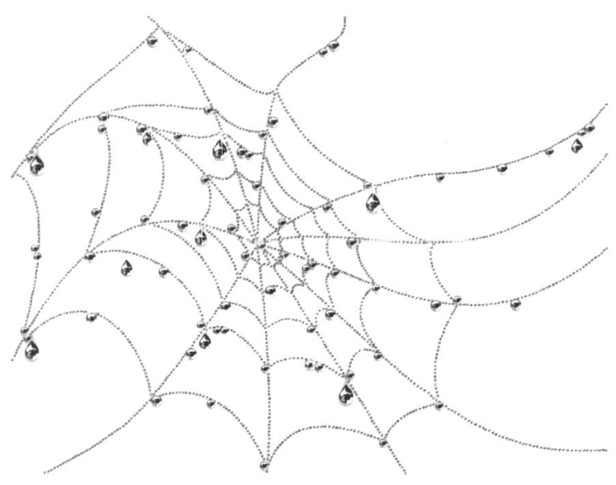

16. Smartwatch

I'd like to ditch the ancient sand-filled hourglass for something more contemporary, like the timer on a smartwatch. A reaper has to stay ahead of his time (pun intended) to remain relevant. A smartwatch featuring timer technology is as effective, if not more so, than the age-old hourglass. An hourglass is at risk for tampering, being flipped upside down just as the final granules drop into the bottom reservoir, extending lifespans indefinitely. This is highly catastrophic. The eternal realm would be less populated and Earth more so. Devastation arises when Earth becomes overcrowded, as folks grapple for land, food, water, and other limited resources.

Nah, a more reliable symbol of the approach to the end of life is necessary. A digital timer that precisely displays the elapse of days, hours, seconds, and even fractions of seconds can't be manipulated to extend life. It's far more accurate than an hourglass, whereby the size of the sand particles and the temperature of the environment impact the rate of flow. Plus, I don't have "time" to calibrate all the hourglasses associated with every life form on Earth. Life is fleeting, and there's no better way to capture its transient nature than through a smartwatch.

I'd set the time of each soul's final moment, then wait for the vibration to rattle my bones. Or I can shake things up a bit and set a particular ringtone when a soul's time has come. In fact, a smartwatch with infinite ringtones would be ideal—one unique sound, perhaps a light whistle or a gentle lullaby, for each soul ready for harvest. Your soul might have its own final ringtone! I can even record my own sounds to use as alerts or dig through my music library. With boundless options, the joys of advanced technology are music to my ear bones!

I'll be sure to trade in the hourglass with which I've been associated for seven centuries too long for a smartwatch. If today's souls wear one, why can't I?

Time's up.

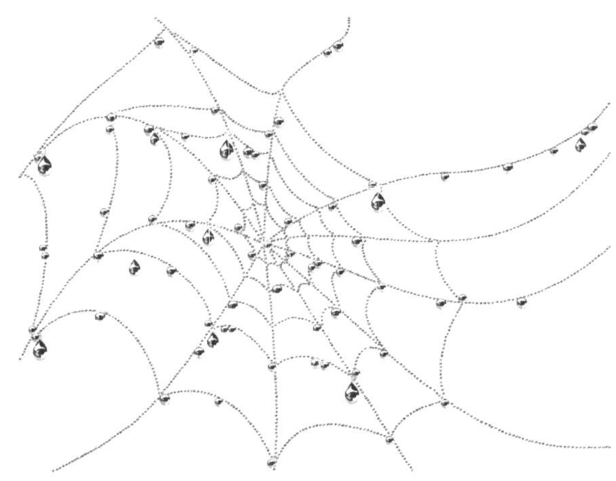

17. Text Alerts

The number one complaint I receive from souls is my premature arrival. They're usually in the middle of something important or unimportant and are not typically happy to see me, even surprised to the point of fainting. Nevertheless, with true grit, I show up, unannounced.

"I was pulling into my driveway, when..."

Or "Eating two hundred hot dogs in ten minutes was only a dare..."

And "I was just trying to get likes."

Folks assume I'm harsh, demanding their souls on the spot, when they're simply out (or in) having a good time. A reaper gets tired of hearing nonstop complaints. No one is ever truly prepared for my arrival. *Sigh*. But I'm a compassionate guy and get how people need a heads up on occasion.

So I've devised a new system. Instead of arriving unannounced, I'd like to propose text alerts. These days, every person on the planet owns a smartphone of some sort, so sending a quick text before their final moment might be a mutually agreeable solution to the universal problem of unanticipated visits. The next world is as old as it gets. But making a minor tech upgrade to accommodate contemporary souls is a worthwhile endeavor.

"I'll be there in ten!"

Or "Expect me after that fifth bottle of tequila."

Short. Sweet. Perfectly reaper.

Isn't that what texting is for?

Sometimes you just need a heads up.

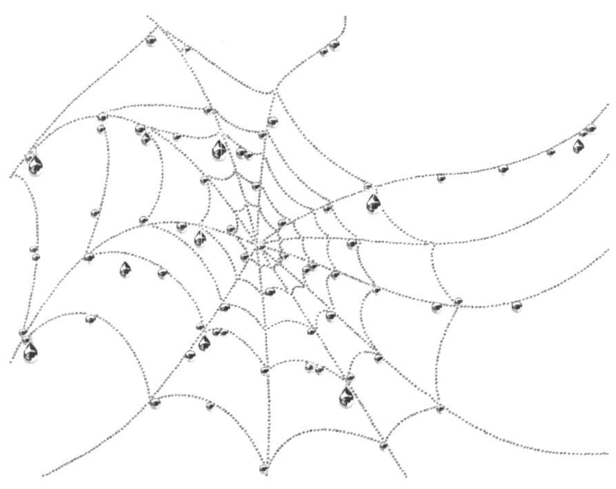

18. Crossbones Pendant

I'd die a second death for a touch of glamour, a bit of bling to make a bold statement, an embellishment to elevate my status to unprecedented heights. I'm the first to admit, sheepishly, that my dowdy appearance fails to deliver the flattering look I set out for all along. It's been this painful way for centuries, contributing to my obvious unease and, likely, the panic with which I inspire awaiting souls. I sort of blend in with the middle realm, being neither here nor there, just everywhere darkness and doom linger. That's a tad gloomy, even for a reaper. Fortunately, the right adornment can whisk me out of my dreary predicament and thrust me into the limelight—where I shine spectacularly like the unrivaled savior I truly am.

I'm thinking a nice, iced-out piece of jewelry, a symbol of success for never having left a soul behind. Something that stands out against my dark style, further forges my unique identity, and makes me the glorious, but taboo, subject of gossip for souls to whom I give safe passage to the other side.

What's that, you ask? A flashy, iced-out pendant in the form of skull crossbones hanging across my rib cage. It'd represent me like nothing else. Even the pirates of yesteryear can't top the dazzling bling I have in mind. Dripping in one carat diamonds and with a thick, silver chain to match, I'd be the talk of the next world.

I'm a blinged-out phantasm you can't unsee.

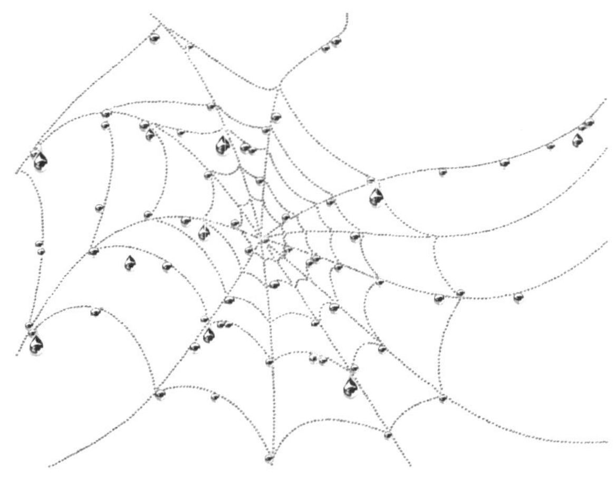

19. Victorian Coach

Death is an honorable transition to the land of eternal light and love—and therefore deserves a mode of transport worthy of this momentous occasion. For centuries, souls have sat morose in my rickety boat, shivering in the corner and fearful of drowning in the cold, murky water, as I rowed them with equal angst to the other side. It's no wonder death has a fearsome reputation.

Each soul is deserving of far more class when they make their final exit. Death is a once-in-a-lifetime event, and souls should go out with pomp and circumstance. We don't necessarily need fireworks displays or elaborate parades—but something dignified.

My mind is whirring with notions of royalty, statesmanship, showmanship—all of which elevate death to the sublime plane it merits. Transporting souls to the other side in an ornate coach would be an upgrade. Perhaps pulled by black stallions, with me assisting as souls climbed up the steps to the velvet interior.

A thin layer of gold leaf would cover the wooden coach. The wheels would be as large as elephants and gilded in gold. I'd have the side panels painted with frescoes of the beauties of the next world. It'd be like a rolling advertisement for the eternal realm. To ensure maximum comfort, a few water bottles and tea bags would be available to all souls upon entrance.

If the souls desire, a hologram of them in their finest year of life would be seen through the windows. Oh, and I'd be driving, leading the horses to the edges of the next world.

A coach to eternity is first-class service, if you ask me.

I don't know 'bout you. But I'd rather hitch a ride to the afterlife in this posh whip over a dingy boat across the River Styx any day.

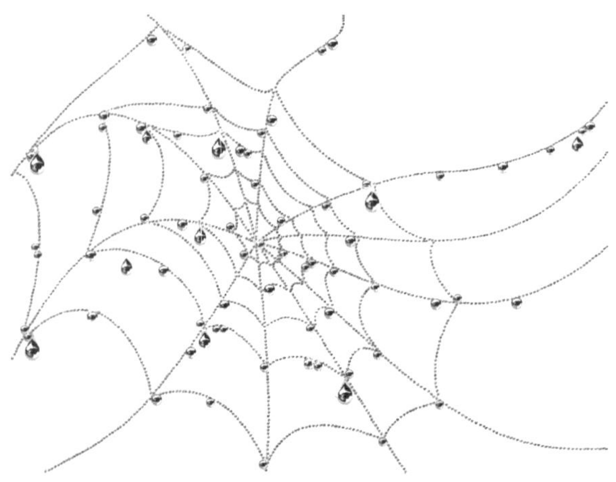

20. Funny Face Eyeglasses

Death is painfully serious. Everyone acts so morosely as I give them passage to the other side. It's a downer having gloomy folks in my boat. Souls need to lighten up. And I've got just the thing! Decades ago, a stand-up comic gifted me a pair of Groucho Marx eyeglasses, with the extra-large schnozzle, big whiskers, and a thick, black mustache. I've kept them tucked in my pocket ever since. I rarely put them on, as souls don't come easily. It's always a struggle getting them onboard that I'm tired out by the end of it and forget. They fear the worst, because death has that kind of fearsome reputation.

Death is wanting of a bit of humor. So I vow to wear my funny face glasses the next time I harvest a soul. Surely, they'd come more readily, seeing the trip to the next world isn't so...dead serious.

Every now and then, I'd swap out my Groucho Marx frames for fake-awake eyeglasses. A pair would soften my fierce, hollowed-out look. Maybe keep the souls guessing! Is he awake, or isn't he?

Next time death is at your door, be prepared for me greeting you with a pair of funny face glasses. It just might brighten up your day. After all, you've just died—and you need a good laugh!

Nothing like Groucho Marx glasses to liven up the dreary trip to the other side.

You can't tell if I'm awake or not, can you.

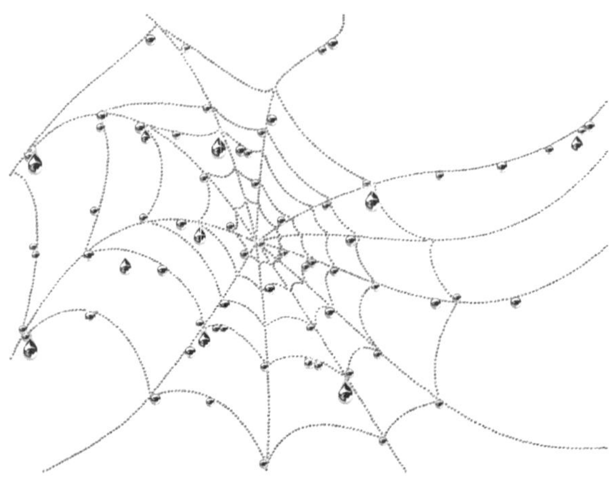

21. Organic White Robe

I've been wearing this tattered black rag for centuries with a gazillion holes to prove it. I'm no angel of death, but I am the deliverer of souls, an exalted position worthy of the highest esteem. Since I transport souls to the land of eternal light, it's fitting that I dress light and airy. It's no surprise I'm considering trading in my black robe for a flowing white one. The color white symbolizes not only new beginnings in the next realm but peace—as all folks "rest in peace" once they make their final exit. I do have to be mindful of my surroundings, though, as a white robe is more susceptible to stains. Washing it frequently is the solution. It's a minor inconvenience, but ensures I present myself as spotlessly as possible to judicious souls.

A white robe made from organic cotton, a gentler fabric than the rough rag I'm used to, is my preference. It's softer, smoother, and feels more luxurious against my bones than conventional cotton. Plus, I'm doing my part for the environment by opting for organic cotton, grown without chemicals and pesticides. I expect my new, organic robe in the whitest of whites to last indefinitely. Organic cotton endures, due to its long fibers, resisting all the wear and tear associated with a harsh job like mine. A few stubborn souls have clawed my original black cloak, tearing it to pieces along the edges, as they struggled to avoid leaving the earthly realm. White, the color of peace, is far more welcoming, so souls are likely to come more amiably. Sporting a flowing, white organic robe makes the process of harvesting souls a more comfortable experience for all. Why didn't my stylist think of this seven hundred years ago?

Waiting for the final moment with billowy grace.

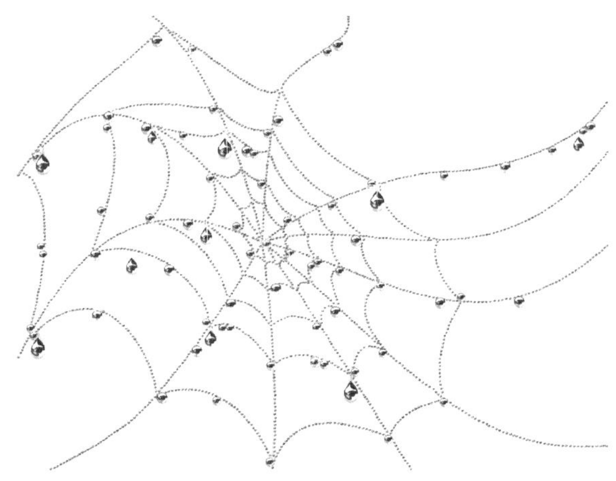

22. Mime

Being a grim reaper is akin to performance art. I rely on silent gestures, intentional skeletal movements, and gory facial expressions to tell the mysterious story of death. Especially upon first acquaintance, I don't say a word to bewildered souls, who are still confused after their soul is promptly severed from their lifeless body. All communication is done by pointing to my boat, the vehicle that takes them to their next destination. A wave of my scythe makes even the most stubborn ones scat toward the River Styx. The magic of it all is that the emotions necessary to play my part effectively are conveyed without speaking. Dread, anxiety, horror—all expressed effortlessly by yours truly. I literally play the part of a mime.

Why not have some fun and actually greet the next soul as one? I'd simply paint my face, *ahem*, it's already ashen white. But I'd dab on a little eye makeup and dress up in a fancy beret, striped shirt, and red suspenders. Creating a visual narrative is as easy as cherry pie. After separating their soul with one slice of my scythe, I'd nod toward the river. Off the soul would go, obedient as a well-trained puppy, hopping into the corner and settling in for a nice, brief journey to the next world. Again, all without uttering one syllable.

It's the resisting souls who spell trouble. Towering over them, I hold the advantage. One stern look with my penetrating hollow eyes and permanent grimace scares even the most dogged folks into doing my bidding—also without one verbal command.

I like the idea of performance art, and serving as the phantasmagoric mime of the in-between realm. It's the way I've performed my role the last seven centuries without realizing it.

My secret? It's all in the silent gestures.

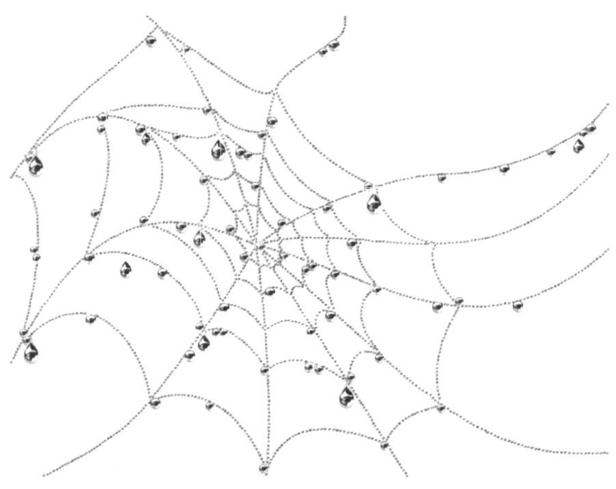

23. Amazon River

The River Styx is no exotic getaway. Dark, cold, and with deep, murky waters, I hesitate to traverse it myself. As a reaper who never learned to swim—and who'd want to learn to swim in the treacherous River Styx anyway—rowing a soul across is a frightful task. But I keep my angst under wraps in these tattered, black layers that hide any concerns I have about the ominous passage.

Certainly, the path to the beautiful afterworld doesn't have to be so frightfully dismal. It's no wonder souls sit silently, hugging themselves and jerking their heads at the slightest sound of the boat creaking or the water seemingly threatening to swallow us whole. I'm thinking to switch things up a bit, find a different way to the next world. I'd stick to a water route, just for the sake of keeping things traditional.

The Amazon River catches my fancy. Surrounded by jungle landscapes and scenic channels, it's my top alternative to the River Styx. At around 4,000 miles, the Amazon is one of the longest rivers. As it's so picturesque, I wouldn't mind lounging on it even in between soul deliveries. Kind of like hanging out at work on my time off. The Amazon is that stunning.

Curious pink river dolphins are known to leap out of the Amazon River, playing with boats that travel across. What a treat they'd be for me as well as the souls to whom I give passage. Souls would look forward to crossing the river—if it happened to be as filled with colorful bird species, stealthy jaguars on the hunt, and other engaging biodiversity as the Amazon River. The River Styx pales in comparison, with not even a mere croak from a toad. It's deathly quiet, eerily foggy, and feels like doom every time I step into the rickety boat. I'd hate to die a second death on the lonesome, isolated, formidable River Styx.

It's time to upgrade the passage to the next realm. I place my vote for the Amazon River. How 'bout you?

The River Styx isn't nearly as stimulating to the senses.

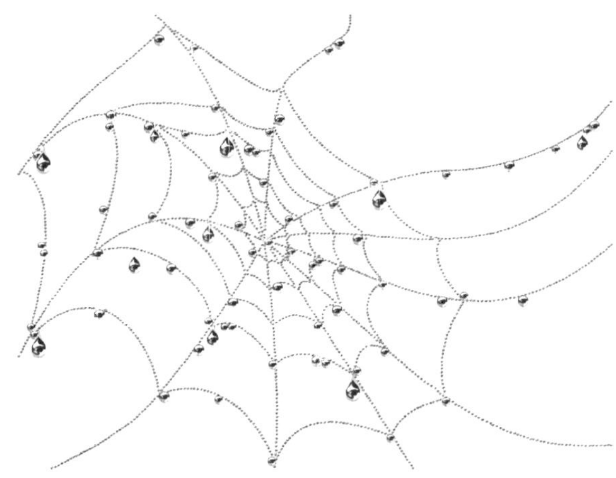

24. Pegasus

If the Headless Horseman can storm the landscape with his horse, I can ride into the sunset on a Pegasus with a soul in tow. I'm sure souls prefer flying across the majestic skies to shivering in a run-down boat that could capsize into the murky River Styx at any unforgiving second.

What better way to honor the wishes of souls than by introducing a Pegasus into the game of death? If a Pegasus can carry Zeus's thunderbolts, it can certainly manage a soul, plus me. With its vast wingspan, it'd soar across the universe and to the next realm in the blink of an eye. The famed wisdom of the Pegasus also makes it the perfect vehicle for helping souls reach the afterlife intact. I doubt the powerful animal would hurl an innocent soul off its back if irked. On occasion, souls test my patience; but I remain the stalwart professional, never giving in to anger and ensuring they reach the next world unscathed.

Plus, the Pegasus is a symbol of freedom—and the eternal realm is as free as a soul can get, ultimate liberation from the weighty chains of life. It's therefore fitting that a soul reaches its final destination on the back of a glorious mythological creature of epic proportions. Death is poetic, and the dead deserve to be transported with elegance.

Enter the Pegasus, a thousand percent upgrade.

Storming across the in-between realm, on my way to collect the next lucky soul!

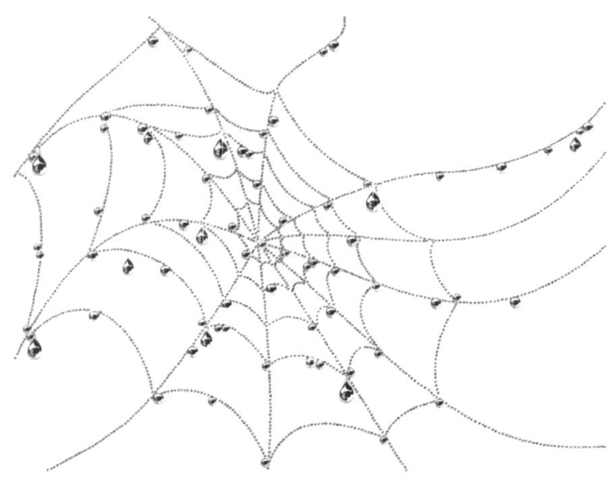

25. Hawaiian Shirts

The afterlife is literally a permanent vacation: joy, light, and love forever after. So why am I forced to dress as if I'm transporting souls to eternal damnation? Come on, the gloomy, black robe, the mysterious hood—it's a getup designed to inspire terror. It's downright unlawful to mislead souls into thinking they're heading toward a portentous fate when, in reality, they're on their way to eternal bliss. I plan on having a word with my stylist, as my current outfit doesn't do me or anyone justice. I need something representing an endless vacay, a nice tropical getaway—like a Hawaiian shirt and coordinating shorts. Add a straw hat, and I'm good to go, as will be the souls who run into my arms, begging me to transport them to the land of light.

A simple swap of clothing makes a world of difference—sending souls running *toward* me instead of *away* from me. Aloha shirts evoke a sense of relaxation, fun, and good times—all glories found in the next realm. If I anticipate an especially important soul on my list, or a scoundrel with a history of mischievous antics, I can easily dress up or dress down. Hawaiian shirts are that versatile.

These vibrant, colorful tops represent peace, goodwill, and love—the quintessential attributes of the afterlife. I consider myself laid back, so these trendy shirts suit me perfectly. Hawaiian shirts, here I come. I aim to stuff my closet full of them. Aloha!

Perfectly represents my laid-back style of existence.

Hey, I'll be your guide to your next destination. No rest stops!

It's made of breathable fabric. Just what I need, alright?

Yep, we're almost there. Eternal getaway, here we come!

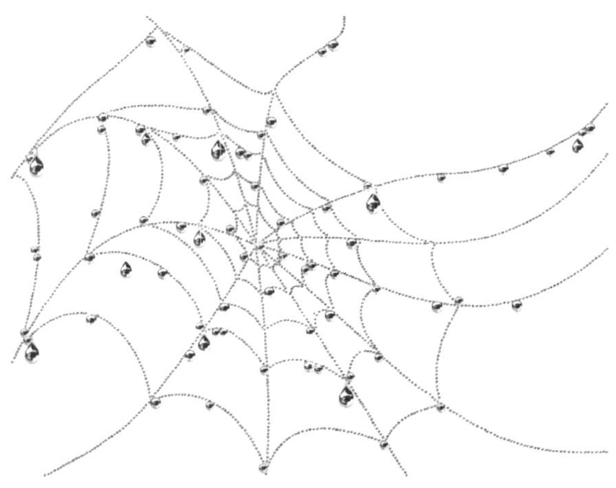

26. Red Convertible

Travel to the next world in style. This isn't just an advertisement. Honestly, who wouldn't want to hop into a gleaming, red convertible, then race, top down, with the breeze blowing through our—*ahem*, your—hair, 'til we reach the edges of the afterlife? Stereo booming, clothes fluttering, and the sun on our skin—and bones! You couldn't ask for a greater final delivery than a hot ride to eternity.

It'd be a thrilling experience to speed off to the next realm, the wheels squealing like there's no tomorrow; for the souls I pick up, there isn't. But eternity surely awaits them. It's the open-air ride of freedom from your tired earthly body, as I cruise with a passion only a reaper can inspire. It'd deliver a sense of unparalleled adventure, maybe even compel souls to bond with me, a dark stud in a sporty car transporting them to everlasting joy. How many souls can say they've ridden shotgun with the grim reaper in a flashy convertible?

None! But I hope to change that with my proposition to ditch my rundown boat and transport souls in a vibrant, red, top-down convertible on the dusty highway to eternity. It offers the best of both worlds!

Self-driving convertible:

the ultimate freedom ride to the other side!

Keep Stylin'!

"The clothes make the man," they say.

"The clothes make the reaper," I argue.

It's about time a professional paid attention to my style. I've gone too long in an outfit that's seen better centuries and with outdated gear. Armed with the polished looks and modernized equipment on these pages, you might be pleasantly surprised upon our initial encounter.

My grand entrance can be either lackluster or magnificent—but as the one-and-only grim reaper, I aim to make a splash.

Until then, stay trendy!

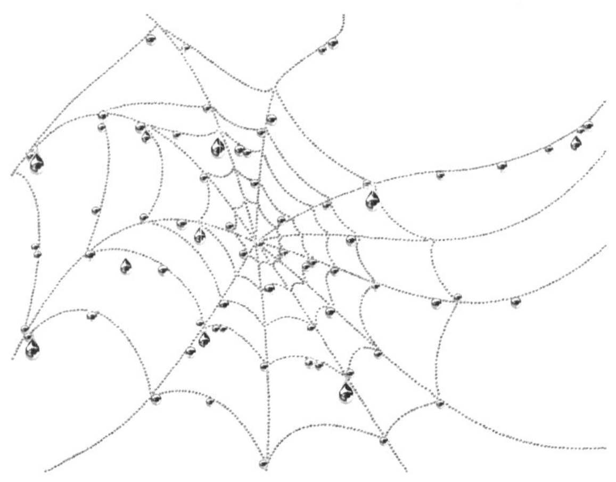

Thank you for flipping through *The Grim Reaper Lookbook*! Did you enjoy perusing the grim reaper's most sought-after styles? If so, he'd be flattered if you shared your thoughts in a retailer review!

www.ingramcontent.com/pod-product-compliance
Lightning Source LLC
Chambersburg PA
CBHW042033180726
48295CB00001B/7

* 9 7 8 1 9 5 6 4 9 6 8 0 2 *